MR.BRAVE

MR.BRAVE
by Roger Hargreaves

Mr Brave is not as strong
as Mr Strong.

He is not as tall as Mr Tall.

But that does not stop him being brave,
as you will soon see.

Now, last Tuesday, Little Miss Bossy invited
Mr Brave to tea.

"AND DON'T BE LATE!" she shouted
down the phone.

It was a very stormy day, but Mr Brave
knew that Little Miss Bossy's temper was worse.

So he set off for Little Miss Bossy's house,
hurrying along as fast as he could
to be sure that he was not late for tea.

Along the way he heard a cry for help.

It was Mr Messy.

He had been blown into the river by the wind.

Mr Brave did not want to be late for Little Miss Bossy
but, being the brave fellow he was,
he jumped in and rescued Mr Messy.

Wet right through,
he hurried along the lane.

Suddenly, he heard someone sobbing loudly.

Who could it be?

It was Little Miss Somersault!

She was balancing on a tightrope
tied between two tall trees!

"Oh, Mr Brave, I'm so lonely," she sobbed.
"Nobody will come and play on my tightrope!
They are all too frightened of heights.
You're so brave, won't you come
and join me?"

Mr Brave looked up at Little Miss Somersault.

Then he thought about Little Miss Bossy,
but, being the brave fellow he was,
he took pity on Little Miss Somersault
and climbed up on to the tightrope.

They chatted away happily for a while
until Mr Brave happened to look down.

"Little Miss Somersault! Look!
The rope is going to snap!
We're going to fall ...
and it's such a long way to the bottom.
Oh, calamity! Oh, help!" he cried out in panic.

"Be brave, Mr Brave," said Little Miss Somersault.

And without more ado,
she carried him safely back
down to the ground.

"Oh, thank you," said Mr Brave,
with a sigh of relief.

Little Miss Somersault said goodbye.

And Mr Brave was left on his own,
shaking like a leaf.

"I don't deserve to be called Mr Brave,
I was scared stiff! Thank goodness
nobody knows my secret,"
he said to himself.

And nobody does know his secret,
or do they?

Little Miss Trouble just happened to be
passing and had seen everything.

And what she had seen and heard
had given her an idea.

A very naughty idea!

She grinned a mischievous grin.

"Hey, come here everybody,
come and see this!" she shouted
at the top of her voice.

Very quickly a large crowd gathered.

"I have an announcement,"
announced Little Miss Trouble.
"Did you know that Mr Brave isn't brave at all?"

"No, it can't be true," said the crowd, all together.

"It is true!" said Little Miss Trouble,
"and I'll prove it to you."

"Mr Brave," she continued,
"I dare you to walk across that tightrope!"

Mr Brave looked up at the tightrope.

And all the crowd looked up at the tightrope.

Then all the crowd looked at Mr Brave.

Mr Brave suddenly remembered something.

A very important something.

"Just look at the time!" he cried.
"I'm going to be late
for tea at Little Miss Bossy's!"

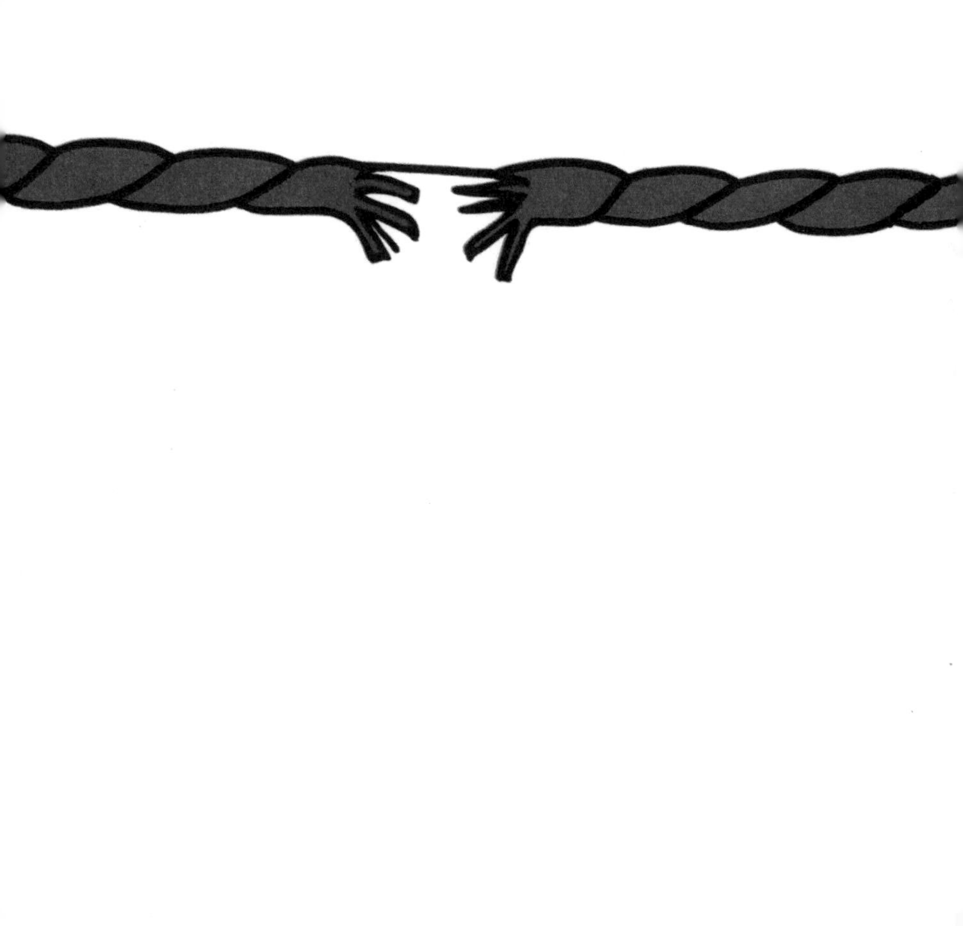

"Must dash!" he cried.

And he ran off as quickly as possible.

"Hooray!" cheered the crowd.

And they all clapped and applauded Mr Brave.

Little Miss Trouble looked puzzled.

"Why are you all cheering him?" she cried.
"He ran away! He isn't brave at all!"

"Oh, yes he is!" they all shouted.
"Would you turn up late for tea at
Little Miss Bossy's house?"

Little Miss Trouble thought for a moment.
"Gosh, he is brave after all!" she said in awe.

Fantastic offers for Mr. Men fans!

Collect all your Mr. Men or Little Miss books in these superb durable collectors' cases!
Only £5.99 inc. postage and packing, these wipe-clean, hard-wearing cases will give all your Mr. Men or Little Miss books a beautiful new home!

Keep track of your collection with this giant-sized double-sided Mr. Men and Little Miss Collectors' poster.
Collect 6 tokens and we will send you a brilliant giant-sized double-sided collectors' poster! Simply tape a £1 coin to cover postage and packaging in the space provided and fill out the form overleaf.

STICK £1 COIN HERE
(for poster only)

Only need a few Mr. Men or Little Miss to complete your set? You can order any of the titles on the back of the books from our Mr. Men order line on 0870 787 1724. Orders should be delivered between 5 and 7 working days.

TO BE COMPLETED BY AN ADULT

To apply for any of these great offers, ask an adult to complete the details below and send this whole page with the appropriate payment and tokens, to: MR. MEN CLASSIC OFFER, PO BOX 715, HORSHAM RH12 5WG

☐ Please send me a giant-sized double-sided collectors' poster.

AND ☐ I enclose 6 tokens and have taped a £1 coin to the other side of this page.

☐ Please send me ☐ Mr. Men Library case(s) and/or ☐ Little Miss library case(s) at £5.99 each inc P&P

☐ I enclose a cheque/postal order payable to Egmont UK Limited for £.................................

OR ☐ Please debit my MasterCard / Visa / Maestro / Delta account (delete as appropriate) for £.................................

Card no. ☐☐☐☐☐☐☐☐☐☐☐☐☐☐☐☐☐☐☐ Security code ☐☐☐

Issue no. (if available) ☐ Start Date ☐☐/☐☐/☐☐ Expiry Date ☐☐/☐☐/☐☐

Fan's name: .... Date of birth: ....

Address: ....

....

.... Postcode: ....

Name of parent / guardian: ....

Email for parent / guardian: ....

Signature of parent / guardian: ....

Please allow 28 days for delivery. Offer is only available while stocks last. We reserve the right to change the terms of this offer at any time and we offer a 14 day money back guarantee. This does not affect your statutory rights. Offers apply to UK only.

☐ We may occasionally wish to send you information about other Egmont children's books.
If you would rather we didn't, please tick this box.

Ref: MRM 001